P9-AOY-578

The Wonderful World of Disney

Walt Disney

SNOW WHITE
AND THE SEVEN DWARFS

DERRYDALE BOOKS
New York

Twin Books

Once upon a time, a beautiful princess named Snow White lived in a castle. But sadly her mother died and her father, the King, soon remarried.

The new Queen was very beautiful, but also very jealous. Everyday she asked her magical mirror:

"Mirror, mirror, on the wall, who is the fairest one of all?"

"You, O Queen, are the fairest in the land," the mirror would answer. The arrogant Queen was pleased, but she feared that Snow White would some day be more beautiful than she. So she made Snow White her servant and gave her old clothes to wear.

But the next day, the mirror said, "O Queen, Snow White is the fairest in the land!"

The Queen was furious. She called her huntsman.

"Take Snow White to the forest. Kill her and bring back her heart in this golden casket," she ordered.

The huntsman took
Snow White to the forest,
but he could not kill her.
The knife fell from his
hand.

He fell on his knees and begged her to forgive him.

"Run away, Snow White, and may the Queen never find you!" he told her.

Snow White ran into the woods. When the night fell, she lay down on the ground and fell asleep. She had very sad dreams.

But when she woke up, what
happiness! All the animals in the forest
surrounded her.

9

The animals tugged at her dress, beckoning Snow White to follow them. They led her to a clearing in the middle of the forest. There stood a lovely cottage.

"Who lives here?" wondered Snow White.

The forest animals smiled happily. They knew who lived there: the friendly Seven Dwarfs!

But the Dwarfs were away working at the mine digging for diamonds and would only be back at night.

The animals gently pushed Snow White towards the cottage. Slowly, she pushed the front door open.

"Oh! Isn't this adorable!" she cried.

"But how messy too!" she quickly added. There were cobwebs in every corner, dust everywhere and a pile of dirty dishes in the sink. "Look! A shoe!" she exclaimed. "I found it in the cooking pot!"

She decided to clean the house before the Seven Dwarfs came back.

Her friends helped her sweep the floor...

...and put everything away...

...and the squirrels dusted
with their thick bushy tails.

13

Meanwhile, the Seven Dwarfs were busy working at the mine. Happy was singing, Sleepy was yawning and Sneezy could not stop sneezing. Bashful, Grumpy and Doc were there too. Dopey had made himself a pair of diamond-rimmed glasses which made his head reel.

Soon it was time to go home. Doc, Grumpy, Happy, Sleepy, Bashful, Sneezy, and Dopey marched out of the mine in single file, singing loudly "Heigh-ho! Heigh-ho!" They were very happy to be going back home.

16

But when they reached the clearing, Doc stopped.

"There's a light in the window!" he cried.
"Who could it be?" the dwarfs wondered.
"If it's a thief, watch out!"

The forest animals chuckled because
they knew who was in the house!

Carefully, the Seven Dwarfs walked to their front door. They slowly pushed it open. What a surprise! The thief had cleaned their house.

"This is a trap," whispered Doc. "Let's go upstairs."

They tiptoed up the stairs and sent Dopey ahead. He gently pushed open the door to their room...

...and closed it just as fast, screaming as if he'd seen a ghost.

"Come on, men!" said Doc firmly.

Nobody said anything, but they all took hold of their picks. When Doc re-opened the door, a huge monster stretched over the beds raised its arms and let out a noisy yawn. All the dwarfs fell flat onto the floor and shut their eyes.

When they peeked out from behind their hands, they were very surprised. The monster was a beautiful young girl! Snow White explained who she was and what had happened to her.

"Oh, please! Could I stay here?" she asked. "I don't know where else to go."

"What an honor!" said the dwarfs. "We'd be glad to have you stay!"

25

Meanwhile, the huntsman had killed a doe and brought back its heart to the Queen. She was pleased.

"I am now the fairest in the land," she announced proudly. She looked into her magic mirror and asked, "Mirror, mirror, on the wall, now who is the fairest one of all?"

But the mirror replied, "Over the seven jewelled hills, beyond the seventh fall, in the cottage of the Seven Dwarfs, dwells Snow White, the fairest one of all!"

"What?" screamed the Queen. "This is not Snow White's heart? Did my huntsman dare disobey me?" She hurled the casket to the ground. "I have been tricked!" she raged. "I will take care of Snow White, and this time she will be gone forever!"

With that, the Queen quickly went down to the castle's cellar.

In an old and dusty book, she found the recipe for a magic potion. She mixed all the ingredients in a glass and, raising it above her head, she said the magic formula, "Abracadabra! Abracadabri! Turn me into an old lady!"

She gulped down the potion. At once, the ground beneath her shook with a thundering sound and her hair seemed to flame. A cloud of thick smoke surrounded her and she let out a scream.

29

The next second the Queen had become a very old and ugly witch. Her nose was crooked and she only had one tooth.

"Let's dip this apple into the magic potion!" she snickered.

"As soon as Snow White sees my apple, so shiny and so red, she will want it!" laughed the Queen. "She will take a bite out of it and fall asleep, but she will never wake up. Never! I will be the fairest in the land then."

The magic potion had only one antidote: love's first kiss. But the wicked Queen was not concerned and left for the forest.

Meanwhile, at the dwarfs' cottage, Snow White was preparing a feast to thank her friends.

"Dinner's ready!" she called. "But let's take a look at those hands before we sit down...."

"My goodness!" she cried with horror. "They are as black as coal! Out we go to wash them at the well!"

When the dwarfs had
washed their hands, they
sat down to eat. The
dinner was delicious!

After dinner, everybody got up to dance.
"What a wonderful partner!" said Snow White to Dopey. Just
then, Sneezy, on whose shoulders Dopey stood, let out an
enormous "A-choo!" and they both fell rolling to the floor!

When morning came, the Seven Dwarfs set out to the mine. Snow White kissed each of them goodbye. Even Grumpy was smiling, won over by her kindness.

"See you tonight!" she called after them as they left.

As soon as the dwarfs left, Snow White started to clean the house.

Knock! Knock! Knock! Someone was at the door. "Who could it be," wondered Snow White. She opened a window to see. An old beggar woman stood outside.

"Have pity on me!" she cried. "I'm hungry! Would you please give me a piece of bread for this apple?"

Snow White nodded yes. But her friends the birds descended on the old woman with fury, trying to scare her away.

"Now behave!" scolded Snow White, pushing them away. She took the old lady inside the house.

42

The birds and the
animals were trying to
warn Snow White. They
chirped and squeaked and
called, "Watch out Snow
White! The old beggar
woman is the Queen!"

But Snow White did not
understand. She gracefully
accepted the apple and
took a bite out of it.

By the time the Seven Dwarfs came home that night, the poison had put Snow White into a very deep sleep. They tried to wake her up, but it was as if she were dead. How sad they were! They gently placed her in a crystal casket and took her to the clearing.

Every day the dwarfs stayed by casket and prayed. One morning their prayers were answered. Prince Charming rode by on his white horse. When he saw Snow White, he dismounted and ran to her. Gently he kissed her. She slowly opened her eyes.

"Will you marry me?" he asked her. When Snow White said yes, the dwarfs sang and danced with joy.

The wicked Queen would never hurt Snow White again. She had been struck by lightning, and fallen to her doom.

The dwarfs and the animals waved goodbye as Prince Charming led Snow White away on his white horse, to his palace high on a hill. There they lived happily ever after.

Copyright © 1988 The Walt Disney Company

All rights reserved. No part of this publication may be reproduced, stored in a retrieval system or transmitted in any form by any means, electronic, mechanical, photocopying or otherwise, without first obtaining written permission of the copyright owner.

This 1988 edition published by Derrydale Books, distributed by Crown Publishers, Inc., 225 Park Avenue South New York, New York 10003

Produced by Twin Books
15 Sherwood Place
Greenwich, CT 06830

Directed by HELENA Productions Ltd

Image adaption by Van Gool-Lefevre-Loiseaux

Printed and bound in Hong Kong

ISBN 0-517-66196-9

hgfedcba

The Wonderful World of Disney